♡ The Owlympic Games ♡

Read more OWL DIARIES

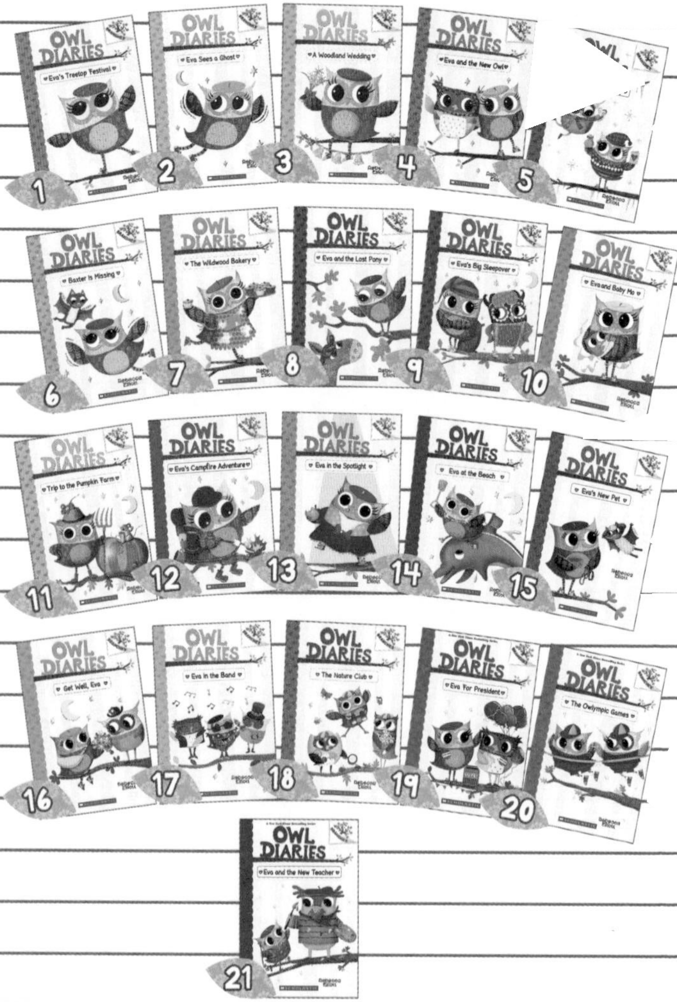

OWL DIARIES
Eva's Treetop Festival
1
Eva Sees a Ghost
2
A Woodland Wedding
3
Eva and the New Owl
4
5
Baxter Is Missing
6
The Wildwood Bakery
7
Eva and the Lost Pony
8
Eva's Big Sleepover
9
Eva and Baby Mo
10
Trip to the Pumpkin Farm
11
Eva's Campfire Adventure
12
Eva in the Spotlight
13
Eva at the Beach
14
Eva's New Pet
15
Get Well, Eva
16
Eva in the Band
17
The Nature Club
18
Eva For President
19
The Owlympic Games
20
Eva and the New Teacher
21

OWL DIARIES

♡ The Owlympic Games ♡

Rebecca
Elliott

BRANCHES

SCHOLASTIC INC.

For all the kids who are great at sports.
And for all the kids who aren't.
You're all brilliant. X — R.E.

Special thanks to Erica J. Chen for
their contributions to this book.

Library of Congress Cataloging-in-Publication Data
Names: Elliott, Rebecca, author, illustrator. | Elliott, Rebecca. Owl diaries; 20.
Title: The Owlympic games / Rebecca Elliott.
Description: First edition. | New York : Branches/Scholastic Inc. 2024. |
Series: Owl diaries ; 20 | Audience: Ages 5–7. | Audience: Grades K–1. |
Summary: Eva Wingdale is excited about competing in the Owlympic Games
at school, but also nervous because in last year's contest she did not
do well—so her brother offers to coach her.
Identifiers: LCCN 2023039238 | ISBN 9781338880304 (paperback) | ISBN
9781338880311 (library binding) | ISBN 9781338880328 (ebk)
Subjects: LCSH: Owls—Juvenile fiction. | Sports tournaments—Juvenile
fiction. | Self-confidence—Juvenile fiction. | Siblings—Juvenile
fiction. | Diaries—Juvenile fiction. | CYAC: Owls—Fiction. | Sports
tournaments—Fiction. | Self-confidence—Fiction. | Siblings—Fiction. |
Diaries—Fiction. | LCGFT: Animal fiction. | Diary fiction.
Classification: LCC PZ7.E45812 Ow 2024 | DDC [Fic]—dc23/eng/20230829
LC record available at https://lccn.loc.gov/2023039238

ISBN 978-1-338-88031-1 (hardcover) / 978-1-338-88030-4 (paperback)

10 9 8 7 6 5 4 3 2 1   24 25 26 27 28

Printed in China   62
First edition, September 2024

Illustrated by Rebecca Elliott
Edited by Cindy Kim
Book design by Marissa Asuncion

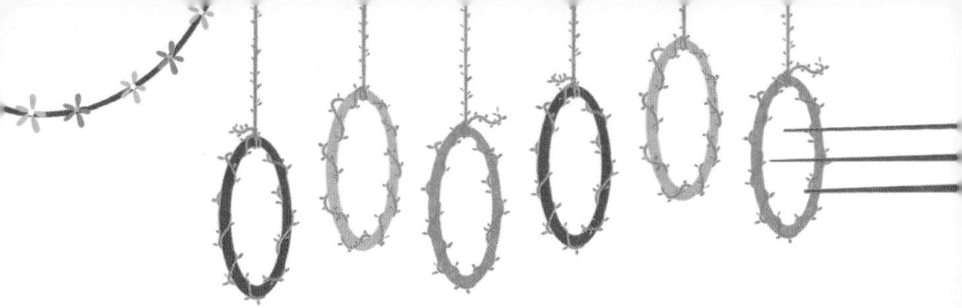

♡ Table of Contents ♡

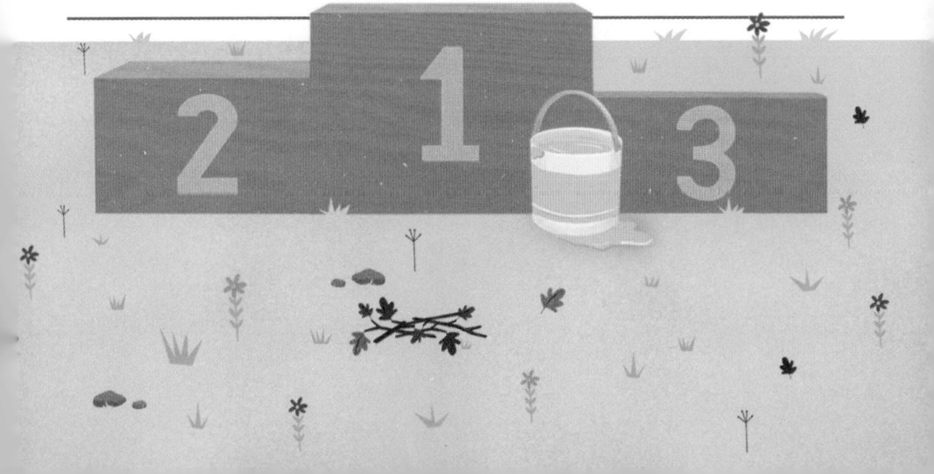

2
1
3

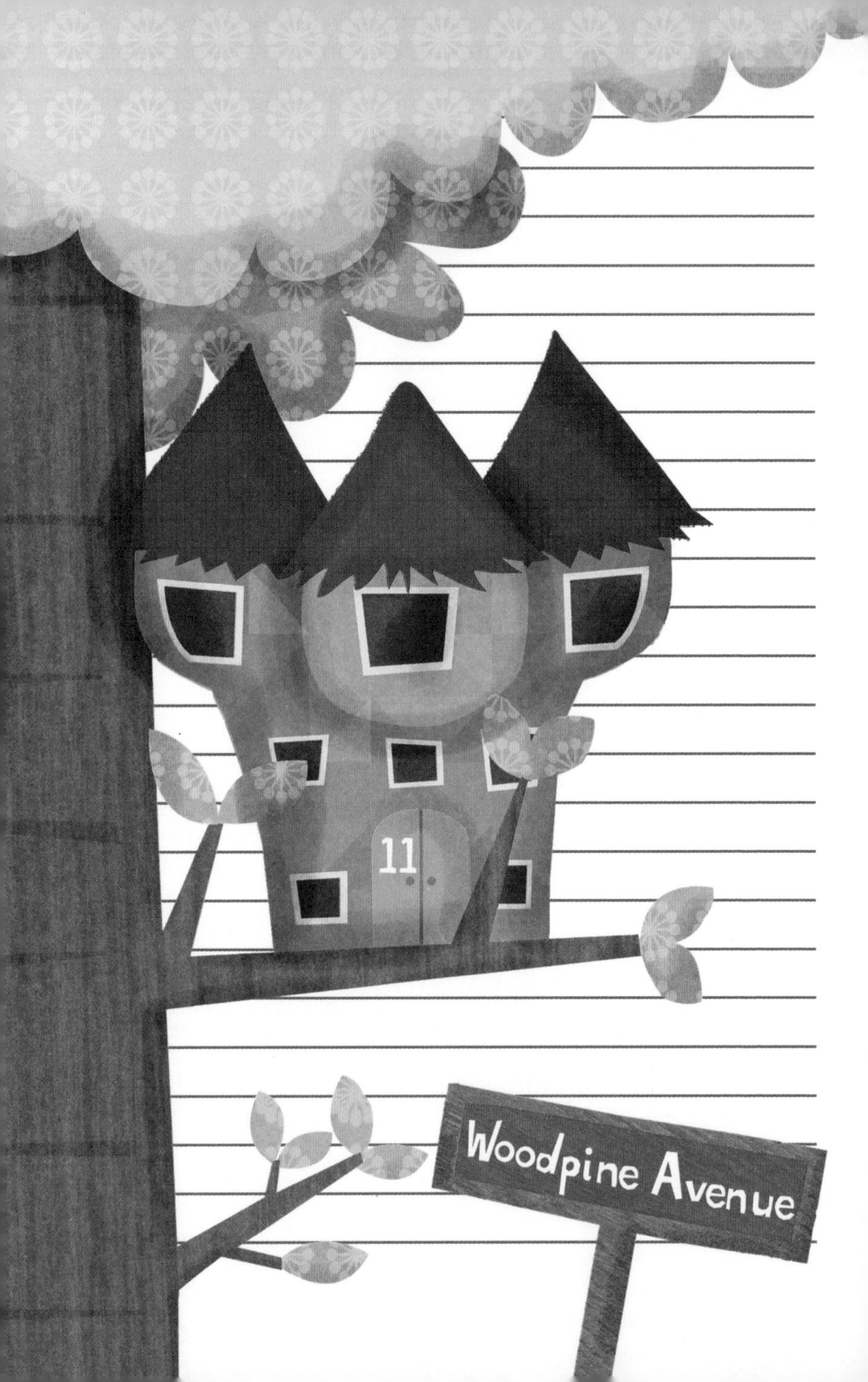
11
Woodpine Avenue

♡ Dreams of a Medal ♡

Saturday

Hi, Diary,

It's me again, Eva Wingdale! The **OWLYMPIC GAMES** are happening at school this week! It's going to be a **FLAPTASTIC** week of fun games and races! I've never won a medal before. Can you imagine if I won one for my team? That would be **OWLMAZING**!!

I love:

Doing my
best to win

Playing team
sports

Crossing the
finish line

FINISH

Cheering for my
classmates

Dreaming big

My new sneakers

Being outside on
a hot school night

The word gold

<u>I DO NOT love:</u>

<u>NOT doing my</u>
<u>best to win</u>

Coming in last
place

<u>Falling before</u>
<u>crossing the</u>
<u>finish line</u>

<u>Not being on the</u>
<u>same team as Lucy</u>

Getting my new sneakers dirty

Embarrassing myself in front of a crowd

Bug bites

The word mud

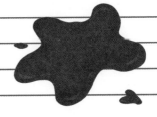

This is my family. We love exercising together! My brother Humphrey is very good at sports. He has won LOTS of **OWLYMPIC** medals!

Mom

Dad

Me

Baby Mo

Humphrey

And these are my pets — Baxter the bat is a very fast flyer, and Acorn the flying squirrel is very good at holding on. We make a great team!

I love being an owl. Owls are good at lots of sporty things.

We can fly fast through tricky obstacles.

We can run fast on the ground.

We're good at balancing.

We can even swim, too!

My family and I live on Woodpine Avenue in the town of Treetopolis. I live next door to my best friend, Lucy.

My friends and I go to Treetop Owlementary School. Here is my class and our teacher:

Mrs. Featherbottom

Jacob

Macy

Zara

Zac

Lilly

Sue

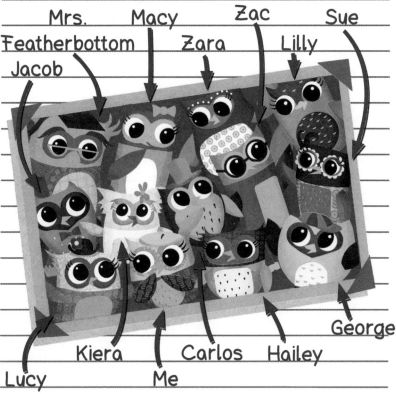

Lucy

Kiera

Me

Carlos

Hailey

George

Oh, Diary, I hope I do well at the **OWLYMPIC GAMES** this week. I feel nervous about competing, so wish me luck!

♡ Coach Humphrey ♡

Sunday

Tonight, Humphrey and I took Baby Mo to the playground.

12

I watched as Humphrey jumped onto the monkey bars.

Wow! I bet you're going to win lots of medals at the <u>Owlympic Games</u> . . . AGAIN! I'm worried about messing up like last year.

Thanks, Eva! I hope we both do well. But this week is not just about winning!

Then why do you <u>still</u> keep your medals from last year under your pillow?!

Yeah, okay. Winning medals is <u>owlsome</u>! Don't worry, you just need some practice.

I flew up to the monkey bars and grabbed on. But I couldn't swing very far, so I slipped and fell flat on my face!

Humphrey jumped up to show me how to swing.

That gave me a great idea.

I know! Can you train me for tomorrow?

Sure, but call me Coach Humphrey. And you also have to change Baby Mo's diapers this entire week.

Hmm, okay. You have a deal!

Great! Let's start with Baby Mo's diaper. It smells BAD!

I changed Baby Mo's stinky diaper as fast as I could.

Then Humphrey blew a whistle really LOUD.

Then we practiced one of the main events of the **OWLYMPIC GAMES**: the pinecone and twig race!

Then he showed me how to cross the monkey bars.

After a couple tries, I got pretty good! So we moved on to some other skills.

Like climbing over a wall.

Flying fast through a set of hoops.

Crawling through a tunnel.

Humphrey really took his coaching seriously!

After that, we practiced the three-winged race. I tied my right wing to Humphrey's left wing to make ONE wing. In this race, we have to fly together with our partner – using only THREE wings!

The trick with this race is to trust your partner.

I took a deep breath and we jumped off a tree branch.

Oh, Diary, this training has not been easy! But I am feeling a lot better because I worked hard tonight. Good night!

♥ Best Owlympics Ever! ♥

Monday

When Lucy and I got to class tonight, we started talking about the **OWLYMPIC GAMES**.

I always get nervous when friends and family are watching.

Me too! Last year, I got so nervous I did really badly in <u>every</u> race. Remember when I dropped the pinecone in the relay race?

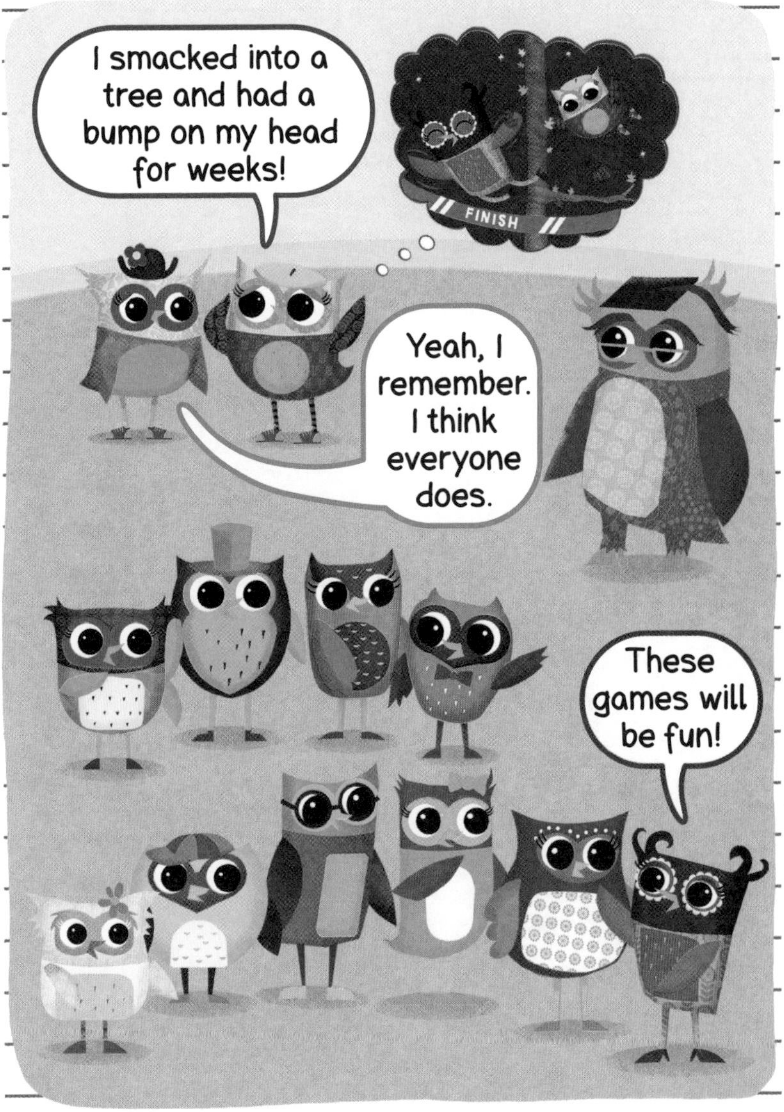
I smacked into a tree and had a bump on my head for weeks!
FINISH
Yeah, I remember. I think everyone does.
These games will be fun!

Mrs. Featherbottom flew over to us.

I felt so much better already.

Soon after, Mrs. Featherbottom made an announcement.

The entire school was getting split into Team Red or Team Yellow, including older students like Humphrey!

Lucy and I wanted to be on the same team really, really badly.

Lucy, Eva, George, Lilly, Kiera, and Zac, you are Team Red.

Yay!

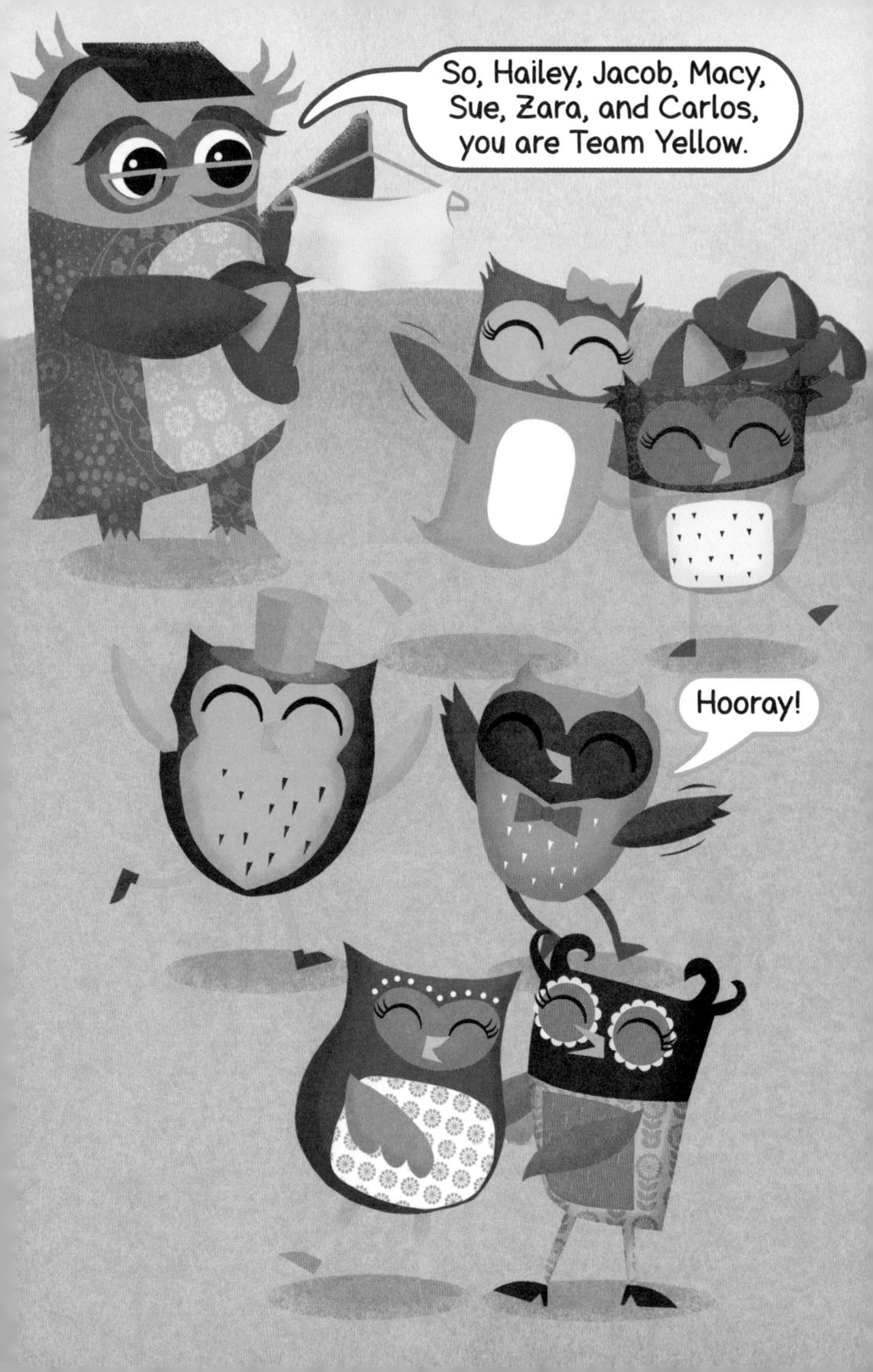
So, Hailey, Jacob, Macy, Sue, Zara, and Carlos, you are Team Yellow.
Hooray!

Sue's comment made my cheeks turn as red as a tomato!

Most of the time, Sue and I get along fine. But sometimes, she's a bit, well, a bit Sue.

As soon as we all put on our team uniforms, I cheered up.

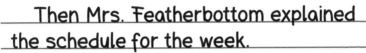

Then Mrs. Featherbottom explained the schedule for the week.

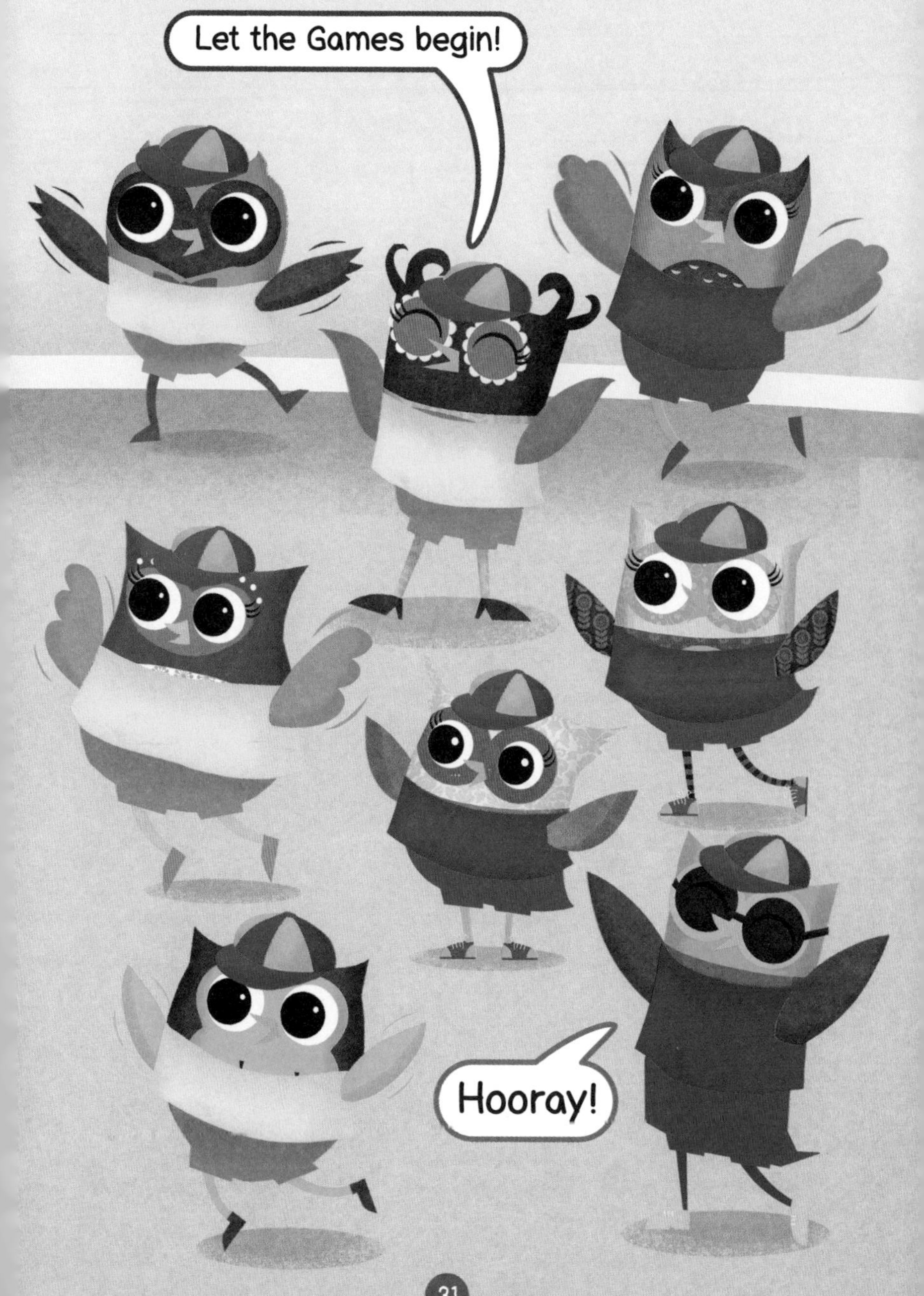
Let the Games begin!
Hooray!

Then Lucy and I spent the rest of the school night setting up for the Opening Ceremony.

We hung the decorations,

made posters,

and set up the game equipment.

We even built a podium. There would be a gold, silver, and bronze winner for each race.

After we finished, Mrs. Featherbottom thanked Lucy and me for doing such a great job.

Then, as a class, we practiced our dance moves for the Opening Ceremony.

And... jazz wings!

It was such a great day, Diary! And I really want to make Team Red proud.

♡ Let the Games Begin! ♡

Tuesday

Tonight we had the Opening Ceremony! First, my classmates and I performed our **FLAPTASTIC** dance routine.

Then our whole school sang the
OWLYMPIC GAMES song.

The <u>Owlympic Games</u> celebrate all kinds of wins! They're about having fun, and stretching our wings.

Now, we were ready to begin the **OWLYMPIC GAMES**! It was time for the first event – the pinecone and twig race!

Okay, get ready! Whoever gets to the finish line first without dropping the pinecone, wins!

START

Good luck, everyone! And most importantly, have fun!

Then Mrs. Featherbottom blew her whistle, and we were off!

We were balancing our pinecones so well. I suddenly felt very confident and sped off even faster!

Before I knew it, I was in fourth place behind Sue!

I was right behind Sue. If I pushed a little harder, I knew I could pass her.

But that's when I noticed Macy's little sister, Mia. She had just dropped her pinecone and she looked upset!

I knew how bad it felt to mess up during a race. So I made a quick game-time decision to turn around.

In the end, Sue came in third, and I lost my chance to get on the podium. Owls from Humphrey's class came in first and second place.

But guess what, Diary? Everyone
cheered for us when Mia and I finished!

Doing the right thing always feels
OWLMAZING!

♥ So Close! ♥

This evening the first event was the twig throw. The goal of the game was to throw a twig as far as we could.

Oh no! I'll be up there by myself with everyone watching!

Don't worry, Lucy. Pretend there's no one else here.

I told Lucy to stretch her wings. I hoped that might help calm her nerves.

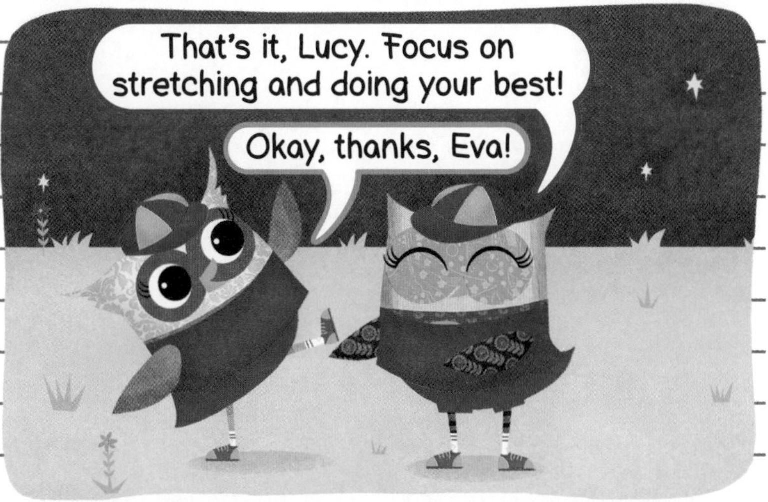
That's it, Lucy. Focus on stretching and doing your best!
Okay, thanks, Eva!

First, Sue took her turn and did a really good throw.

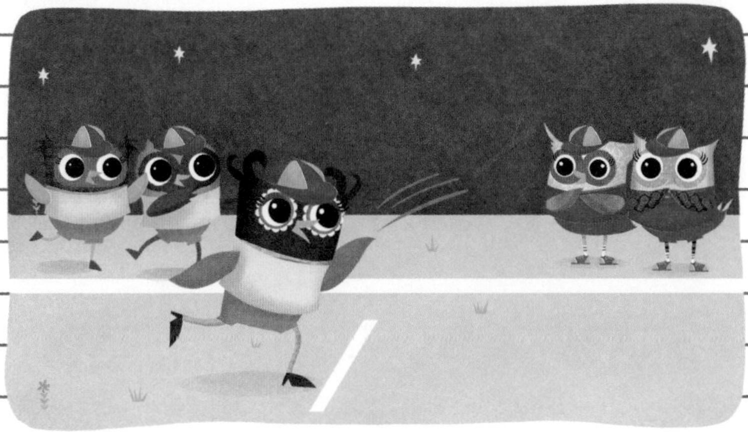

Then it was Lucy's turn! She chose her twig and flew up in front of the crowd.

Then she threw her twig as far as she could. It went even farther than Sue's!

I was so excited for Lucy that I forgot
to warm up before it was my turn.

I threw the twig as hard as I
could . . . but it didn't go far at all! It
was SO embarrassing. But when I saw
Lucy smile at me, I felt much better.

Soon, everyone finished throwing. Then Mrs. Featherbottom announced the winners.

And guess what, Diary? Lucy won a SILVER medal and Humphrey (who is also on Team Red), won GOLD!

Yay! Go, Lucy and Humphrey!

I saw Mom and Dad cheering in the crowd. Suddenly, I really wanted to win a medal and make them feel proud of me, too.

Luckily, I still had a chance to help my team win! The next event was the sack race. The goal of this game was to bounce to the finish line as fast as possible. This time, I made sure to warm up!

Then we lined up and climbed into our sacks.

Mrs. Featherbottom blew the whistle and we were off! Lilly, Zac, and two of the older owls fell over right at the beginning. Everyone looked so funny!

Carlos started off strong and quickly took the lead. But then he fell, and two of his teammates tripped over him, too!

I knew that now was my chance to get ahead. So I kept bouncing toward the finish line!

I looked behind me. Lilly, Zac, and a few older owls were back in the race, too. Sue was getting closer. And suddenly, she was hot on my tail!

But this time, I was so fast — I knew I could finish. Until . . . DISASTER!

I fell flat on my face as my sack got caught on a tree.

I didn't win. But guess what? My teammates rushed over to help me. We bounced over the finish line together – laughing the whole time!

Oh, Diary! I was SO close to winning! But I'm not giving up on helping my team because tomorrow is a new day!

♡ Don't Let Your Team Down! ♡

Thursday

Tonight's big game is a **FLAPTASTIC** obstacle course. Before the race started, Coach Humphrey pulled me aside.

But after watching a few players fall, I started getting nervous.

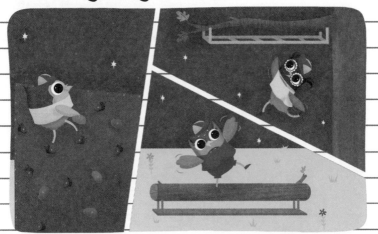

This was a timed race. So right before my turn, Mrs. Featherbottom reset her stopwatch and blew her whistle. And with that, I was off!

It all started out well. I crossed the monkey bars quickly.

I walked across the balance beam.

I climbed over the acorn rock climbing wall.

I breezed through all the hoops.

Then I heard Humphrey cheering from the ground.

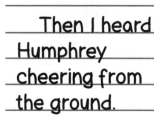

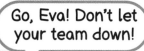
Go, Eva! Don't let your team down!

Suddenly, all I could hear in my head was, "Don't let your team down!" over and over again. Before I knew it, I lost focus and didn't know which way to exit the tunnel.

Then I heard Humphrey yell again.

WRONG WAY! TURN AROUND, EVA!

So I flew back the right way and finished the race. I had made a BIG mistake, so I knew I'd lost my chance at getting a medal again.

You might have made a mistake, but you were SO fast! And don't worry, there's still one more game tonight: the team relay race!

Humphrey was right — we still had one last race tonight. Four owls per team were racing. We each had to fly one lap around the Old Oak Tree before passing the pinecone to a teammate.

This time, Humphrey was competing with me!

Now remember, the most important thing in the relay race is . . .

To stretch! And of course, DON'T DROP THE PINECONE!

Oh, Diary, that's exactly what I did last year! No matter what, I CANNOT drop the pinecone!

Our team did really well from the start. Then, when it was time for me to fly my lap, I grabbed the pinecone from Humphrey.

Then it was me against Hailey. I flapped my wings as fast as I could. But as I turned the corner, I bumped into a tree branch . . . and dropped the pinecone.

Oh no!! Not again!

But that's when Hailey swooped down
and caught it!

Hailey gave me a little wink.

Then she quickly flew ahead of me
and finished first.

Soon, Humphrey rushed over, too.

You know what, Diary? Humphrey is probably right. But I don't want to have to change who I am to win! I'm happy to be a good teammate.

Tomorrow is already the last day of the **OWLYMPIC GAMES**. I can't wait to find out which team wins!

7

♡ HOO Wins? ♡

Friday

The winning team will be announced at the Closing Ceremony tonight.

But first, it was time for the three-winged race. It was the very last race of the week.

Okay, everyone. Find a partner and tie your wings together!

I knew there was no one I wanted to do this race with more than Lucy.

So we tied our wings together, jumped off the tree, and started flying. Fast!

Soon we were up in the front!

And GUESS WHAT, DIARY?

This time, WE WON . . . TOGETHER!!

I gave Lucy a big hug. I couldn't believe we had won a gold medal. It was a dream come true!

And thanks to our win, Team Red won the team trophy at the **OWLYMPIC GAMES**!

I really helped Team Red win the games!

I jumped up and down with all of my teammates.

Team Yellow was happy for us. They cheered loudly, too!

When the Closing Ceremony began, we got a surprise. Every player on both teams was given a shiny medal for **OWLSOME** team effort . . . including me!

That's when Mom, Dad, and Baby Mo found me and Humphrey. We shared one big **OWLSOME** hug.

This was the best **OWLYMPIC GAMES** ever! Whether you win or lose, you can always be kind and be a good sport. See you next time, Diary!

Rebecca Elliott was a lot like Eva when she was younger: She loved making things and hanging out with her best friends. Now that Rebecca is older, not much has changed — except that her best friends now include her two sons, Benjy and Toby. She still loves making things, like stories, cakes, music, and paintings. But as much as she and Eva have in common, Rebecca cannot fly or turn her head all the way around. No matter how hard she tries.

Rebecca is the author of several picture books, the young adult novel PRETTY FUNNY FOR A GIRL, and the bestselling UNICORN DIARIES and OWL DIARIES early chapter book series.

OWL DIARIES

How much do you know about The Owlympic Games?

Reread chapter 2. According to Coach Humphrey, what is the most important thing to do before playing any sports?

 Lucy is nervous about competing in the Games. What is she nervous about and what advice does Eva give her? Reread pages 22 and 44.

Reread chapter 3. What is the goal of the <u>Owlympic Games</u>, and what will happen at the Closing Ceremony?

 During the pinecone and twig race in chapter 4, Eva needs to make a quick game-time decision. What does she decide to do?

Lucy and Eva pair up for the three-winged race. According to Lucy, why do they make a good team? What are Lucy and Eva finally able to achieve together? Reread pages 66–67.